MY ADVENTURES

WITH

This book was especially written for
Bennett Lyon
with love from
Grandma Sue

Adapted by Kate Andresen

ISBN 978-1-875676-28-6

The Case of the Missing Spatula

SpongeBob met Mr. Krabs at the front door of the Krusty Krab.

"Ready to fry up a lot of Krabby Patties today, SpongeBob?" Mr. Krabs asked.

"Ready as ever, sir!" SpongeBob shouted. "And so is Flipper!" He held up his carrying case.

"That spatula has made me a lot of money... I mean, patties," Mr Krabs said, opening the front door.

SpongeBob cheerfully greeted his fellow employees as they arrived for work.

"Morning, Squidward! Morning, all!" called SpongeBob. "Today is a special day. I'd like you to welcome Bennett Lyon to the Krusty Krab. Bennett is visiting us from Fairfax City."

"Hello everyone!" said Bennett.

"I'm really excited to be here! I'm looking for somewhere to hold my birthday party on February 3rd and I've heard that the Krusty Krab has the best Krabby Patties in Bikini Bottom. Only the best will do for Matthew, Lexie and Jack!"

They went through to the kitchen to set up. Mr Krabs opened the kitchen door and yelled, "There's a big school of hungry kids out here. Start flipping those Krabby Patties, SpongeBob!"

"Right away, Mr. Krabs! But first I need my trusty Flipper," SpongeBob answered as he opened his case. But the case was empty. "Jumping jellyfish! Flipper has gone! I can't fry without him!" SpongeBob screamed.

Just then Patrick came in. "Hey, SpongeBob!" he called. "I've been waiting for you at Goo Lagoon! We're gonna make sand castles, remember?"

"Patrick, my spatula is missing!" cried SpongeBob.

"You can't work without your spectacles!" cried Patrick.

"Spatula," corrected Bennett. "Don't worry, SpongeBob. I'll help you. We'll be detectives. First, we'll question the witnesses."

"Good idea, Bennett!" replied SpongeBob. "Squidward, what do you know about the missing spatula?"

"Nothing!" replied Squidward.

"And you, Mr. Krabs? What can you tell us about Flipper's disappearance?" SpongeBob asked.

"All I know is that without Flipper, there are no Krabby Patties, which means no customers and no money!" shouted Mr. Krabs.

"OK, Mr. Krabs. We're on to it!" said SpongeBob. "If there are no witnesses, we must question the suspects."

"But who would want to keep you from making Krabby Patties?" asked Bennett.

"Health experts?" suggested Squidward.

"Crimes connected to Krabby Patties usually get traced back to one person: Plankton," said Mr. Krabs.

They ran to the Chum Bucket and burst through the door. Plankton jumped to his feet.

"Hot dog!" he yelled. "Customers!"

"Not customers," SpongeBob said. "Detectives! Give me back my spatula!"

"Yeah! Give back SpongeBob's spectacles!" Patrick shouted accusingly.

"Spatula, Patrick," said SpongeBob gently.

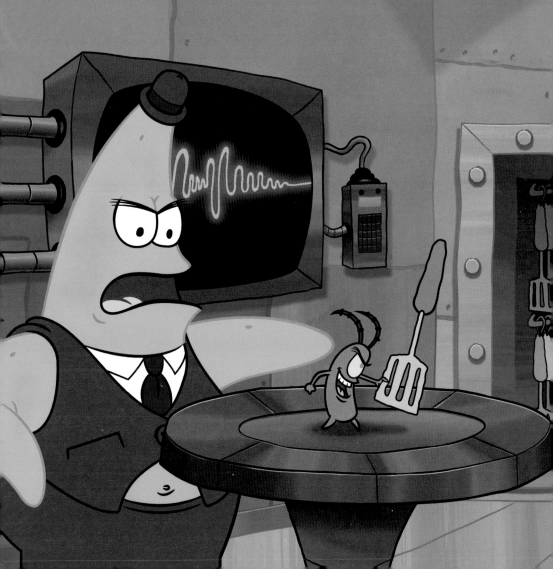

"Why would I take your spatula when I've got plenty of my own?" replied Plankton pointing to his rows of spatulas.

"He's got a point. But if Plankton didn't take Flipper, who did?" Bennett wondered aloud. "I know… it's usually the person you least suspect! SpongeBob, who do you suspect less than anyone else in the world?"

SpongeBob thought long and hard. "Sandy?"

"To the treedome!" cried Patrick.

Sandy was outside hanging out her washing.

"Sandy, you haven't seen my spatula, have you?" asked SpongeBob.

"You've lost Flipper? That's terrible, SpongeBob!" said Sandy shaking her head. "I haven't seen it."

Bennett, Patrick, and SpongeBob searched through Sandy's yard, but there was no sign of Flipper.

"Where were you yesterday?" Bennett asked.

SpongeBob scratched his head and thought for a minute. "I was at Mrs. Puff's driving school," he said.

"OK, let's go and see whether you left Flipper there," said Bennett.

But Mrs. Puff hadn't seen SpongeBob's spatula either.

"Think, SpongeBob. Where did you last see it?" asked Mrs. Puff.

"At my house," he said. "I always sleep with it as it helps me dream of Krabby Patties."

"Then it must be there. Why don't you go home and check?" suggested Mrs. Puff.

They ran to SpongeBob's pineapple.

"I always put Flipper in his case and lay it on this trunk," SpongeBob said.

Bennett inspected the trunk. "What are those dark smudges?" he asked.

SpongeBob wiped his finger over one of the smudges. "Mmm… it smells like chocolate! It tastes like the ice cream Patrick and I ate last night!" exclaimed SpongeBob.

Bennett pointed to some prints by the trunk. "Those look like footprints… round footprints! I wonder where they lead to?" he said.

"Let's follow them," said SpongeBob. "It's fun being a detective!"

They followed the footprints all the way to Goo Lagoon.

"Oh boy!" said Patrick. "The beach! We can build sand castles!"

"Patrick, we're looking for my spatula, remember!" Suddenly SpongeBob spotted a familiar handle sticking out of the sand. "Flipper, what are you doing here?" cried SpongeBob as he pulled out his beloved spatula.

"That's my digger, that's not Flipper," said Patrick. "I was using it to make sand castles. I borrowed it from your house last night."

SpongeBob hugged his favorite spatula.

"Oh, Patrick!" laughed Bennett. "So you're the one who took Flipper."

"You were right, Bennett! It was the person I'd least suspect," smiled SpongeBob. "We'd better get back to the Krusty Krab. I'm going to make you the best Krabby Patty you've ever tasted, Bennett. And you, Matthew, Lexie and Jack are welcome at the Krusty Krab any time."

Back at the Krusty Krab, Mr. Krabs stuck his head round the kitchen door and yelled, "Ready for some hungry customers, SpongeBob?"

"I'm ready! Flipper's ready! We're all ready to go!" shouted SpongeBob.

That day SpongeBob made the best batch of Krabby Patties he'd ever made.

The Case of the Vanished Squirrel

It was a windy day in Bikini Bottom. SpongeBob was staring out the window.

"Hey, Patrick, let's go see if Sandy wants to blow some bubbles with us and watch them blow away in the wind," SpongeBob suggested.

"Hey! What!" Patrick said, waking suddenly from his nap.

On the way over to Sandy's, SpongeBob and Patrick bumped into Bennett, Matthew, Lexie and Jack.

"Hey, we're going to get Sandy then go and blow bubbles. Why don't you come with us?" asked SpongeBob.

"Sounds like fun!" replied Bennett.

There was a note pinned to Sandy's door which SpongeBob read out loud. "It says: 'I've taken.'"

Bennett picked up another piece of paper off the ground. "This one just says: 'Sandy'".

"Oh, no! Someone's taken Sandy!" cried Patrick.

"She's been squirrel-napped by whoever wrote this note!" cried SpongeBob. "This is another case for SpongeBob DetectivePants and his assistants.

"OK everyone! Let's comb the ground for clues!" SpongeBob announced.

They searched everywhere and soon SpongeBob spotted an acorn cap.

"Aha! Do you know what this is?"

Patrick squinted at the acorn cap. "It looks like a tiny hat," he suggested.

"It's the top from one of those nuts Sandy eats. She must have dropped it when she was squirrel-napped!" said SpongeBob.

"Look, there's a trail. Let's follow it! I'm sure it will lead us to Sandy," Bennett said. "Keep a lookout for other clues."

They followed the trail to Mussel Beach, where they found Larry the Lobster munching on acorns.

"Where did you get those?" SpongeBob asked suspiciously.

"Sandy gave them to me the other day, after her morning workout," Larry answered.

"You squirrel-napped her, didn't you?" Patrick accused.

"What are you talking about, dude!" said Larry. "We worked out and then she left."

"Let's form a line and move up the beach. That way we won't miss anything," suggested Bennett. They continued searching the sand for clues.

After a while, Patrick noticed something in the sand. "Look, Mr. DetectivePants. What's this?"

"Hmm," said SpongeBob, studying it carefully. "It looks like an eye patch. The kind worn by pirates!"

"But there aren't any pirates here, are there?" asked Bennett. "It probably belongs to some kids."

"I have heard of pirates hanging around these parts," interrupted SpongeBob.

"You mean, like the Flying Dutchman?" asked Patrick.

"Exactly! He must have dropped it when he took Sandy to his ghostly ship!"

"But how do we find his ghostly ship?"

"Isn't that it, right there?" Larry said, pointing.

Bennett, Matthew, Lexie and Jack followed
SpongeBob and Patrick up a rope to the Flying
Dutchman's ship. They tip-toed across the deck,
trying not to make any noise. But Patrick tripped
and knocked over a barrel.

"Sssh!" whispered Bennett.

Suddenly, the Flying Dutchman appeared in front
of them and roared "Who dares to board my ship without
permission?"

"We-we-we're looking for my-my friend Sandy. She-she's a squirrel," stuttered SpongeBob.

The Flying Dutchman looked puzzled, "Who's Cindy?"

"Yeah, SpongeBob, who is Cindy?" asked Patrick, confused.

"Not Cindy, *Sandy!* She's my friend, and she's a squirrel!"

"What squirrel? Squirrels aren't allowed on my ship! Now off with you all!" growled the old pirate as he tossed them overboard!

They landed on the sand with a THUD.

"Oh boy, that was one mean pirate!" said Patrick as he brushed the sand off his clothes. "But if the Flying Dutchman didn't take Sandy, who did?"

"I don't know, Patrick," replied Bennett. "Perhaps we should go back to Sandy's house to see if we missed any clues."

They began to walk home slowly, still scouring the sand for more clues.

SpongeBob looked discouraged. "Maybe I'm not such a great detective after all."

"You're the best detective I've ever worked with," said Patrick loyally.

"Thanks, Pat," said SpongeBob.

When they got to Squidward's house, they heard a terrible noise! It sounded like someone yelping!

"Maybe it's Sandy!" cried SpongeBob.

SpongeBob and Patrick burst through Squidward's door, followed closely by Bennett, Matthew, Lexie and Jack.

"What's this!" exclaimed Squidward. "I'm practicing my clarinet."

"You're under arrest, you squirrel-napper!" yelled Patrick.

"Oh dear!" exclaimed Bennett. "That's not Sandy yelping. It's Squidward playing his clarinet."

"Hey, Squidward, when was the last time you saw Sandy?" asked SpongeBob.

"She was here a few days ago. You weren't home so she asked me to tell you that she was going away. I would have told you sooner, but I've been busy playing my clarinet," replied Squidward.

"Where did she go when she left here?" SpongeBob asked eagerly.

"To the Bus Station!" answered Squidward. "Now get out of my house!"

They arrived at the bus station just in time to see Sandy getting off a bus.

"There she is!" cried Bennett. "She's safe."

They all ran over to Sandy and she greeted them with a big smile and said cheerfully, "It sure is nice of y'all to meet me here!"

"Sandy, where have you been? We thought you'd been squirrel-napped! We found these on your door," SpongeBob cried out excitedly, waving the scraps of paper at her.

BUS STOP

"Slow down, little buddy!" Sandy said as she looked at the scraps of paper.

"Hmm, the wind must've torn up my note. It actually read: 'I've taken a trip to Texas fer the annual Horn-Lockin' Competition. Back soon, Sandy.' Thanks for trying to find me though."

"You're welcome, Sandy," answered SpongeBob.

He looked at all his friends and announced, "I, SpongeBob DetectivePants, officially call this case closed!"

For our entire selection of books, please visit www.identitydirect.com

This personalized SpongeBob SquarePants book was especially created for Bennett Lyon of 3705 Mason Street, Fairfax City with love from Grandma Sue.

Additional books ordered may be mailed separately — please allow a few days for differences in delivery times.

If you would like to receive additional My Adventure Book forms, please contact:

My Adventure Books

PO Box 5057
Des Plaines IL 60017-5057
Phone: 1-888-586-1600
www.identitydirect.com

0 3 7 2 0 0 4 4 1 7 0 0 0 1 0 1